Stone

a rat's tale

Write to Stacey Stone – the Agony Aunt who really is an Aunt!

All your problems solved – guaranteed!

Well, I'll have a go, anyway...

Dear Stacey,
Please, please, please tell me how to get out of going to Brownies! I don't think I can stand it any more!

Yours,
A very sick Pixie, Year 4

Hmmm, no problem.

Dear Stacey,
How can I get hold of Myleene from Hear'Say's phone number? She's purely gorgeous and simply a babe!

From a desperate fan, Year 8

How sad is this guy? I bet I know who it is...

Look out for Stacey's next big crisis...

Cooking Up Trouble

Stacey Stone

a rat's tale

Roy APPS

This edition produced for the Book People Ltd,
Hall Wood Avenue, Haydock, St Helens WA11 9UL

First published by Scholastic Ltd, 2001
This edition published by Scholastic Ltd, 2005

ISBN 0 439 95487 8

Printed and bound by Norhaven Paperback A/S, Denmark

The Incredible Shrinking Boy!

The day my life changed for ever, scientists in America were working on a pill to help you live to a hundred and fifty, and a lorry driver in Portsmouth was attempting to break the World Burping record.

I know this, because I was watching *Wake Up World!* on breakfast TV whilst chomping my way through a bowl of Whizzo Wheat and trying hard not to think about the awful day I'd got ahead.

After the news, Trudi Truelove appeared on screen. She's *Wake Up World!*'s agony aunt. She's dead good. She helps people sort themselves out.

"Hello, I'm Trudi Truelove, the agony aunt with attitude, and next on the line is Sheryl from Sheffield," she said, a look of grave concern spreading across her face.

A crackling voice came down the line into the studio. "Hello, Trudi? It's my boyfriend, Arnie. He's moved out and set up home with Charlene."

"And is Charlene your best friend?" asked Trudi.

"No," sobbed Sheryl from Sheffield, "Charlene's my goldfish."

Trudi blew her nose into a big hankie. "That is so sad, Sheryl!"

Soon Sheryl from Sheffield was pouring out her heart to Trudi Truelove, me and about two million other viewers. I wondered if I should write to Trudi Truelove. Surely she'd be able to help me with my problem.

I pushed my Whizzo Wheat to one side and grabbed a pen and paper:

Dear Trudi

My name is Stacey Stone from Dunbridge. I'm twelve (just) and I try to be kind to animals and people and I tidy my room when I remember. I have a problem to do with my best and only friend Ali. She moved to London with her mum. Now it's the first day of term and I have no friends. No one to sit next to. No one to have a laugh with about boys. No one to share my most embarrassing fantasies with. Life without Ali is going to be awful. What can I do?

Stacey Stone

Trudi Truelove would be able to sort it all out, I was sure. I could just imagine the scene. The door would burst open and she would be standing there with Ali, saying:

"*Stacey, darling! Look who's here!* Wake Up World! *has arranged for you and Ali to have six weeks of sun, surfing and all-night discos in Florida!*"

Right on cue, the kitchen door burst open.

But it wasn't Trudi Truelove, it was my mum. And she was on the warpath.

"Stacey, you'll be late for school!" she shouted. "Shove that disgusting pap down your throat and get a move on. I've left your PE trainers in the hall, your Food Tech apron in the airing cupboard and your packed lunch in the fridge."

"Thanks, Mum," I sighed. She plonked a lip-sticky kiss on my forehead.

"Have a good first day of term, love. And don't worry! I know you're missing Ali, but you'll make new friends." She's brilliant, my mum. She's got a full-time job at the Do-Less

DIY Superstore, but she always manages to get everything ready for us.

"See you later!" she yelled.

"Bye, Mum!" I called as the door slammed shut behind her.

On the telly, Trudi Truelove was still talking to Sheryl from Sheffield. "Sheryl darling, will you promise me you'll tell your Arnie he's got to grow up and choose between having a relationship with a goldfish or with you?"

"Thank you, Trudi," said Sheryl. "I will! You've really helped me, you know!"

I tipped the rest of my soggy Whizzo Wheat down the sink and went in search of my stuff. I found my trainers in the fridge, my Food Tech apron in the hall and my packed lunch in the airing cupboard. Like I said, Mum always manages to get our stuff ready for us. The trouble is, she doesn't always get it ready in the right place.

I traipsed upstairs to the bathroom. The door was locked.

"Lena, how long are you going to be in there?" I shouted.

"What's it to do with you?" came the reply.

"Nothing, only I've just seen a great, fat, hairy spider crawl under the door."

"Yeah, right," said Lena, obviously not believing me. Lena's my sister. She spends ages in the bathroom. She's trying to make herself look beautiful, which is an amazingly difficult job. She's fifteen. Though when she went into the bathroom, she was only fourteen and a half.

"But I need the loo!" I said, desperately.

"Use the downstairs one, then," came the reply.

"Thank you very much! I hope you get a really zitty spot right on the end of your nose," I called back as I trudged downstairs.

I hate the downstairs loo. It's got a plastic seat that you stick to if you sit on it for too long. The bathroom's got a wooden seat. And a shelf full of books to help pass the time.

Ten minutes later, I slouched off down the road to school. Normally, I'd call for Ali on the way, but today I was on my own. I wondered how *she* was feeling on the first day of term at her new school.

I'd just posted my letter to Trudi Truelove in the box on the corner of Cranberry Crescent when I was confronted by a truly horrible sight. It was a sight so horrible there were only two words to describe it: Ed Reekie. His trousers hung round his ankles like a pair of concertinas.

His sweatshirt drooped halfway to his knees. You couldn't see his hands, but the tips of his fingers dangled from his sleeves like cows' udders. He was eating a banana.

"Ed, what happened?" I said. "Was it the sun?"

"What?" said Ed.

"Made you shrink? Was it too much sun?"

"Oh, very ha ha," scowled Ed. "I haven't shrunk. It's just my mum's bought me new clothes. She says they've got to last me right through Year 7."

"Yeah, and Year 8 and 9 too, by the look of it," I said, stifling a giggle.

"She says I'll grow into them," he muttered.

"I've heard of an ugly duckling growing into a beautiful swan, but never of a boy growing into a pair of trousers," I replied.

"Oh, ho," said Ed, which is what he always says when he's trying to pretend that one of my jokes isn't rib-ticklingly funny.

Suddenly, he started peering hard at the space next to me. Then he peered behind me.

"What?" I asked, feeling a little uncomfortable. "You do know it's rude to stare?" Nervously, I checked to make sure that I hadn't tucked my skirt into my knickers by accident. But everything was in place.

"She really has gone, then," said Ed.

I felt the knot in my stomach tighten. "Who?" I asked him, though I knew perfectly well who he meant.

"Ali."

"Yeah. She moved down to London with her mum."

"You two were almost inseparable, you know," he went on. "I bet you feel a bit weird, don't you?"

I didn't say anything.

"Who are you going to sit next to in class, now?" asked Ed.

"Not you," I replied, quick as a flash.

"That's a relief," he said.

I shot him one of my withering looks. I don't normally let a boy cheek me like that, but unfortunately, I've known Ed a long time. We were at playgroup together, and he knows too many terrible secrets about me for me to get on the wrong side of him. Well, you wouldn't want the whole class to find out about the time you wet your knickers in the Nativity Play, would you?

We walked on to school in silence. This happens a lot when you're walking along with Ed, because his mouth's always full of food. He never stops eating. He's all right really, I suppose. He must be, otherwise I wouldn't still be talking to him after all these years. It's a shame he's a boy, otherwise we'd probably be best friends.

As we reached the school gate, he raced over to greet Lee Queng. "Awright pal, eh?" he yelled. Then Lee Queng punched him on the shoulder so hard that he almost fell over.

If Ali had been with me, we would've creased up laughing.

Yes! It's Another Monday at Doris Grundy!

School smelled like the first day of a new school year; all floor polish and new paint.

We marched into the hall and sat cross-legged on the floor. The teachers stood behind us, like prison guards. This week's assembly music blasted out of the speakers. It sounded worryingly like a funeral march, which I suppose was very appropriate for the first day of term. Then the music stopped and Spooky Pooky, our head teacher, strode up to the front of the hall.

"Good morning, Doris Grundy," he boomed.

Doris Grundy was not the name of a person, you understand, but the name of our school. The Doris Grundy Middle School, to give it its full title.

"Good morning, Mr Pook. Good morning everybody!" we chorused back.

"Welcome back! I trust you all return to school suitably refreshed and regenerated after the long summer break. This term," Spooky Pooky droned on, "I want everybody –" he paused, and pierced a fidgety Year 6 boy with his laser-gun eyes – "and everybody includes you, Jason Lurkin, to get their heads down and put their noses to the grindstone."

I wondered just how painful it would be, having your head down while your nose was being ground on a grindstone.

Spooky Pooky spent ten minutes telling us what he didn't want to see around the school this term: litter, fighting, make-up, Man U shirts and people kissing behind the pig-swill bins. Then he spent the rest of assembly telling us what he didn't want to *hear* around the school this term: screaming, shouting, fighting, swearing, singing.

After assembly, we trudged off to our classes. This year, I was in Ms Angel's class, which was cool. Ms Angel is fantastic. She only started teaching two years ago and she's the only teacher in the entire universe who's heard of Westlife *and* Ronan Keating. She's got a Morris 1000 convertible called Flossie and a boyfriend called Jerome.

Everyone rushed to find a seat. Boys near the windows, girls next to the wall. I found myself looking round for Ali. I couldn't help it.

The seat next to mine was empty. But not for long. I looked up and saw Joanne Jobbins with her hand on it. She flashed me a big bright smile.

"Mind if I sit here, Stacey?"

I was about to tell her I'd rather have Hannibal Lecter sitting next to me than her, but didn't get time to open my mouth before she continued, "Only you must be feeling lonely now that Ali's gone."

Then she sat down.

A word about Joanne Jobbins, aka "Odd" Jobbins. That's the word – *odd*. Last year, she followed Heidi Buckmaster about, as if she was her shadow. I had a dreadful feeling that this year, it was my turn.

My worst fears were confirmed when Joanne got out her pencil case. It was a Westlife one, just like mine.

Ms Angel took the register, then said, "Right 7A, before we get down to work, I'd like to tell you about this year's exciting special project."

There was a big groan. Last year's "special project" had been Recycling. This had involved bringing rotting cabbages to school and chucking them into a big green bin. Exciting? Not.

Ms Angel held up a crumpled sheet of paper.

"This, as you can see," said Ms Angel, "is a copy of The Doris Grundy Middle School newsletter, *The Grundy Times*. Until now, of course, it has been written entirely by various members of staff. But I think this school needs something better, like a proper newspaper. And I've managed to persuade Mr Pook to give a group of pupils the chance to run *The Grundy Times*."

Us? Running a newspaper? I couldn't believe it! Being award-winning journalists was something Ali and I had always planned we'd do together. I was going to do the words, she was going to take the pictures. But we'd always thought we would have to wait until we got our English GCSEs.

I put up my hand. "What sort of things can we put in it, miss?" I asked.

"As it's a newspaper, might I suggest you start with news?" replied Ms Angel, smiling.

"Is there going to be a page three girl?" asked Ryan Grummett, his tongue hanging out.

There were excited whistles from the boys. Ms Angel raised her hand for quiet.

"No, Ryan, there certainly is not," said Ms Angel, firmly.

There were disappointed groans from the boys.

"So, are there any volunteers?" asked Ms Angel.

"Me, miss," I yelled. "Miss! Me, miss, miss! Me! Me!"

Joanne saw my hand go up and immediately put hers up, too. It was obvious that anything I did, she was going to do, too. What a copycat!

The only other person with their hand up was Ed. Then I saw he wasn't actually volunteering. He'd dropped a pen down his shirt sleeve and was trying to waggle it out. Given the length of his sleeve, this was a major operation.

"Three ... well, it's a start, at any rate," sighed Ms Angel, looking a little disappointed. "Stacey, Joanne and Ed, can you come along to the practical area at lunch time. There's a meeting with the editors."

"Who are the editors, miss?" I asked. I'd rather hoped I might have been made editor myself.

"Natalie and Matthew from Year 8," said Ms Angel.

"Nat 'n' Matt?" I repeated in horror.

"Nat 'n' Matt?" echoed Joanne.

"Gotcha!" said Ed, shaking the pen from his sleeve on to the floor, and still blissfully unaware that he'd just signed up for a year's-worth of hard-hitting investigative reporting.

The Day My Life Changed For Ever!

A word about Natalie and Matthew, as Ms Angel called them, or Nat 'n' Matt as everybody else calls them. Simply, they think they're Doris Grundy's answer to Posh and Becks. Talk about fancying themselves. They make *the* Posh and Becks look like a pair of shrinking violets. Just because *he* can kick a football without falling flat on his face, and *she's* got these eyes as dark and round as Wagon Wheels.

All right, *he's* captain of the school football team, and *she's* dead pretty (in a *thin* sort of way).

At 12.30pm prompt, *The Grundy Times* editorial team assembled in the practical area; me, Ms Angel, Ed, Joanne and Nat 'n' Matt. Five of us; or six if you counted Nat 'n' Matt as two people. Nat shrank away from us, like we were diseased persons.

"Do we *have* to have these *tweenies* helping us, miss?" she asked, pouting.

"I am not a *tweenie*!" I retorted. "I am twelve – and a week."

"I'm twelve and seven-and-a-half-months," Nat retorted.

"Girls!" interrupted Ms Angel, "less of this ageism, please. And to answer your question Natalie, yes, Stacey, Joanne and Ed are going to be helping write *The Grundy Times*. They're going to learn the ropes, so that they can run the paper when you and Matthew go to Upper School next year."

I screwed up my nose and gave Nat a ner-ner look.

Joanne smiled approvingly at me. Ed was munching his way through a slice of pizza.

"Now," said Ms Angel, "Natalie and Matthew are going to edit the paper and I shall keep an eye on proceedings to make sure everything's running smoothly. Joanne, Stacey, Ed, have you thought about what jobs you might like to do?"

I certainly had. During Literacy Hour I had done a lot of thinking about what I would write for *The Grundy Times*. I had finally decided on an opinion column, offering my thoughts on all the important issues of the day, like whether Hear'Say were a better band than S Club 7 (no) or whether Mr Griddle, who taught IT, was the lushest teacher in the school (yes).

"I'd like to write an opinion column called 'Stacey Stone Speaks Her Mind'," I replied.

"You might like to, but you're not going to," growled Nat. "Who do you think would be interested in the opinions of a Year 7? And anyway, there's only one place for opinions in *The Grundy Times* and that's *my* leader column."

"I do take Natalie's point on this one," said Ms Angel. "Her leader column will provide us with all the opinion we need, I'm sure. Is there anything else you'd like to do on the paper?"

I looked at the floor. I could think of plenty of things I'd like to do with Little Miss Smuggy's column – and none of them were printable.

There was an embarrassing silence. "Well, let me throw a few ideas into the pot," said Ms Angel, pulling out a little list from her bag. "For a start, we'll need someone to run the Swap Shop column."

Running the Swap Shop column was the one job I definitely did *not* want. But I shoved up my hand. Joanne saw me and quick as a flash shoved her hand up, too. I waited a few seconds, then I pulled my hand down. Joanne wasn't quick enough. Her hand stayed up just long enough for Ms Angel to see it.

"Joanne! Well done! I'm sure you'll agree that it'll be a very worthwhile column!" said Ms Angel, beaming.

"But I don't really want..." stuttered Joanne. I shot her a pleasant smile.

"Now, Natalie," said Ms Angel, moving swiftly on, "as Stacey isn't able to write an opinion column for the paper, have you got any thoughts about what she might do?"

"She could help me run the Swap Shop column," suggested Joanne.

"That's very thoughtful of you, Joanne," said Ms Angel, "but I think one person running the Swap Shop column is enough."

So did I.

All the while, Nat said nothing. She twiddled a ringlet of hair round her finger and stuck out her bottom lip in a big pout.

She made me seethe. Just for a minute, I wished I was Trudi Truelove, *Wake Up World!*'s agony aunt. I'd tell Miss Fat-alie-Natalie.

Natalie darling, would you promise to do something for me? Promise you'll go and shove your head into a saucepan of soup?

And then it hit me. An idea which was so brilliant I don't know why I hadn't thought of it before.

An idea which was perfectly suited to a sensitive, mature and intelligent human being like me.

An idea which would change my life for ever. I would be *The Grundy Times*'s answer to Trudi Truelove!

"Actually," I blurted out. "I'd like to do a problem page."

Ed started choking on his pizza. He *may* have got a crumb stuck in his throat, of course, but from the astonished look he gave me, I suspect he found the idea of me running a problem page rather hard to swallow. A bit like his pizza, in fact.

"A problem page! That *is* a good idea, Stacey," said Ms Angel, brightly. "You could be *The Grundy Times*'s own agony aunt!"

"No, she couldn't!" snapped Nat.

"Why on earth not?" Ms Angel asked her.

"She's only Year 7!"

"So?" I said.

"Year 7's don't know anything!"

"I'm the *oldest* Year 7 in the school," I replied, huffily. "And not only that, I am actually an aunt." This was true, my other big sister, Lindsey, who's twenty-one, and her partner Darren, have got a baby called Liam Darcy Wiggins.

I produced a photo of Liam Darcy from my bag.

"Ooooh, isn't he sweet!" cooed Ms Angel, suddenly going all mumsy. Liam Darcy has that effect on people. Joanne craned her neck to have a look at the photo, too. Ed, being a boy, didn't bother.

"A problem page would be dead boring!" said Nat.

"Yes!" agreed Matt, loyally.

"You'd have Year 4's writing in with stupid problems like 'How can I stop my jam sandwiches going soggy?' " added Nat.

"Do you *know* how to stop jam sandwiches going soggy?" I asked.

Nat didn't reply.

"There you are then!" I answered, triumphantly.

"Yes!" echoed Joanne. "There you are."

"I don't care! It's *our* paper and we're the editors!" declared Nat. "And we get to decide what goes in it!"

Ms Angel glanced up from studying Liam Darcy's photo and frowned. "Excuse me. It's the *school* newspaper and I'm the member of staff responsible for it," she said, firmly. "I suggest that Stacey tries her problem page for a few editions. And we'll review the situation in a month's time."

"Thank you, miss," I beamed.

Nat pouted some more. Joanne smiled.

"Now, Ed," said Ms Angel. "Any ideas?"

"What?" said Ed. He was still trying to work out just how he came to be in the practical area at the very first editorial meeting of *The Grundy Times*.

"About what you want to do on the paper."

"Er ... Foreign Correspondent?" suggested Ed. I think that somewhere in the spongy matter inside his head that passed for a brain, he was expecting Ms Angel to give him a return ticket to Sydney or New York or somewhere.

"Wally," said Matt. "How would you ever find your way to anywhere foreign? You even got lost on your Cycling Proficiency Test and that was just round the school grounds."

"Actually, it's not a bad idea," said Ms Angel.

"It would do us all good to be a bit more aware of what is happening in the wider world around us. I'm sure Ed will be able to find some very interesting stories. Good! Now everyone has a job and knows what they're doing. I'm sure you'll all strive to make this a super team effort, and I look forward to reading the draft copy of what I know will be a brilliant first edition!"

And with that she skipped off to the staff room to do the kind of things that teachers do in the staff room: eat, sleep, drink coffee and gossip, gossip, gossip.

THE GUARDIAN
MASSIVE HUNT ON AS GOVERNMENT LOSES CRUCIAL VOTE
THE SUN
SOAP STARS IN LOVE ROMP !!!
ARE THEY BONKERS?
THE DAILY MA
ENGLAND WI
ANOTHER MATC
1,000s DIE OF SHOC
THE GRUNDY TIMES
NAT 'N' MATT GET GOOD WORK AWARDS
GOOD WORK AWARD
GOOD WORK AWARD

4 The Girl With The Ear-Nibbling Boyfriend

Ms Angel let us use the practical area as *The Grundy Times* editorial office. She said it was the ideal place, in case we made a mess. I think she was thinking of all the blood there would be on the carpet if Nat had another go at me and I aimed a punch at her perfect nose.

It was really cool. We had a computer – on line – use of the school camera, a dictaphone for interviews, our own letterbox and a whole wall for clipping up photos and page mock-ups. There was a phone as well, and Mrs Dickens in the school office said she'd switch any calls for

The Grundy Times through to us. Outside, next to the door, was *The Grundy Times* noticeboard. I'd already pinned up a note asking people to contact me with their problems.

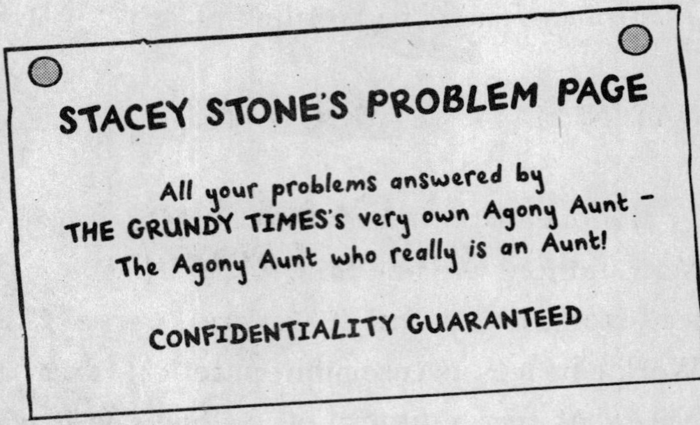

On Thursday, Nat 'n' Matt called an after-school meeting to discuss the "dummy" first edition. Ed and I mooched along. Ed was eating a cereal bar.

"Have you grown at all?" I asked him, looking at his baggy uniform.

"Oh, ho," he replied.

"Oh, you are wicked, Stacey!" trilled Joanne, who was walking about a metre behind me. She had been following me around as if she was joined to me by an invisible thread of superglue. I opened the door to the practical area. Ed and Joanne followed me in. On the noticeboard was a mock-up of the dummy first edition of *The Grundy Times*. The headline read:

NAT 'N' MATT GET GOOD WORK AWARDS!

I looked from the wall to a grinning Nat 'n' Matt. If there was one thing to be said about this lead story, it was that it was *true*. Large "Good Work" badges were pinned to Nat 'n' Matt's shirts.

It amazes me that they still give out "Good Work" badges in Year 8. You would have thought they would be above that sort of thing. If *I* do any good work when I'm in Year 8 – I said *if* – I shall ask for something more useful than just a "Good Work" badge – perhaps a backstage pass for the next Robbie Williams concert.

I took another look at the noticeboard.

"I know it's a dummy first edition, but that doesn't mean it has to have a dummy headline," I said. "This isn't news."

"Why, have any of you tweenies come up with something better?" snapped Nat.

"I've got a Swap Shop item!" said Joanne with pride. She took a slip of paper from her bag. "For Sale: Pair of ice skates, £2. Very good condition." She paused. "One missing."

"Riveting," said Matt, sarcastically.

"Yeah," Nat agreed. "That should really excite any one-legged Eskimos who happen to read the paper. And what about Auntie Stacey's Problem Page?" she sneered. "Has anyone come running to you for your expert advice?"

I gave her one of my withering looks and pulled out a small file.

"I've had a letter from a girl in Year 4 who wanted to know how to get herself banned from the Brownies," I said. "I sent her the usual advice."

Nat affected a yawn. "Boring," she said.

"Then I had a letter from a boy—"

"What advice?" demanded Nat.

"Oh," I said. "I wasn't going to tell you. I thought you'd find it boring."

"We're the editors," Matt chimed in, "we've a right to know of any correspondence that goes out from this office."

"I told her to replace the Brownies' Pixie chant with the following little ditty," I explained.

"I'm a little pixie,
A-dancing on my log.
I hope a hunky lad walks by,
'Cos I'm dying for a snog."

Joanne guffawed. "That's awful, that is! Real good," she said. "You *are* clever, Stacey."

"Yes, I am, aren't I," I replied. Joanne looked hurt. Ed shot me a disapproving look. OK, perhaps that was a bit *too* sarcastic, but I was getting really fed up with her trying to pretend she was my best friend. Ali was my best friend. And Ali was gone.

"You said something about a letter from a boy," Nat said, icily.

"Oh yes, I've not had a chance to reply to him. He wanted to know where he could get hold of Myleene from Hear'Say's phone number."

Nat shivered. "Urgh. What a saddo! I hope you tell him he's a creepy little perve."

"Matt, you're a creepy little perve," I said.

Ed burst out laughing. Joanne just looked amazed. Matt went as red as a tomato. "How ... how did you know it was me?" he stuttered.

I was about to tell him all about my brilliant female intuitive powers, when Nat started thumping him about the head.

"You're a lech, Matt Pascoe!" she screeched.

Matt covered his head with his hands. He's very protective about his head. Not because he's got anything in it, but because he scores so many goals with it.

I decided it was time to play my trump card. I went over to the computer and casually announced, "I did get this desperate email from a girl in Year 8, though." I tapped into my personal mailbox and read:

"*Dear Stacey Stone's Problem Page, Last night my dad caught me in my bedroom with Brad...*"

I looked up. Just as I'd thought. Ed, Joanne and Nat 'n' Matt's eyes were all pinging out of their sockets like party poppers. No one said anything.

"*He was nibbling my ear at the time,*" I continued. "*Oh, he's such a cutie! Anyway, my dad says that if he ever finds Brad in the house again he'll bundle him into a sack with a couple of house bricks and chuck him in the river. Please, please help me!*"

There was a silence which lasted about an hour. Then Joanne said, "Wow!"

"Some story, eh?" I said.

"Do you really think her dad's going to chuck Brad in the river?" Joanne asked.

"He might," I said, trying to sound knowledgeable.

"Or he might not," said Ed. "My dad once threatened to chase me to hell and back, but he never did. For a start, he didn't know the way—"

"Ed," I interrupted, "this girl's dad's made a threat. I've got to take it seriously."

I glanced at Nat 'n' Matt. I almost felt sorry for them. They sat there, trying desperately not to be excited.

"Right," Nat said, trying to keep calm. "This sounds like our first big story. We'll need some pics." She picked up the camera and dictaphone and headed for the door.

"Hang on a minute, I'm coming too," I protested. "It's *my* story!"

"Yeah, it's Stacey's story!" chimed Little Miss Echo.

"Don't you think you should talk to this girl first?" said Ed. "Find out what's been going on?"

"Look," I told him, "when someone comes to you in time of trouble, they don't want someone to talk to; they want action!"

Ed shrugged. "If you're sure," he said.

"Nat! Nat! Wait for me! I'm coming!" whined Matt.

"If you're sure you're not too busy trying to get hold of ladettes' phone numbers," retorted

Nat, waspishly. I *love* it when those two row. It's such fun.

I joined Nat at the door. "Nat," I said. "You can't go without me."

"And why not?" pouted Nat.

"Because *I'm* the only one who knows this girl's name and address," I replied.

Who Is Marcia Boggart!

The girl with the ear-nibbling boyfriend hadn't signed her e-mail, but there was an e-mail address: trubshawe@freemail.com. There was only one Trubshawe at The Doris Grundy Middle School; her first name was Zoe. She was a flirty little madam with eyes like cornflowers and ears like cauliflowers. She'd been dating older boys since the Infants. Which was why, I presumed, none of us knew her bloke Brad. He was obviously at the Upper School.

Nat 'n' Matt strode out in front, Ed and I followed behind them and Joanne brought up the rear.

"Who are you planning to interview?" I asked. "Zoe won't want her story plastered over the front page. She'll want to remain anonymous."

"I might talk to the officer in charge of the murder investigation," replied Nat.

"There hasn't been a murder, yet," Ed reminded her.

"And once Stacey's sorted things out, there won't be any need for Zoe's dad to chuck Brad in the river," added Joanne, helpfully.

"That's a pity," sighed Nat, "because a murder would make a really cool front page story."

"What a ghoul!" Ed whispered to me, chomping his way through a packet of raisins.

The Trubshawes' house was on the corner of a cul-de-sac on the old estate. It had a high hedge at the front. Ed, Joanne, Nat 'n' Matt and me crouched down behind it, trying to blend in. It didn't work, though. Soon, people walking past started to give us funny looks.

"It's OK," I said to them, "we're doing a school project." They seemed happy with that.

Matt had the camera's telephoto lens trained on the front door. Nat was saying "Testing, testing, one, two, three," into her dictaphone. Then they looked at each other. It seemed the row was now off, because they looked at each other again – and again and again and again. Soppy, lovey-dovey looks which made me feel very sick.

Suddenly, the Trubshawes' front door swung open and a surly-looking man appeared. I say "man", but he made The Incredible Hulk look human, he was that huge. He could have gone on *Stars In Their Eyes* as the Grinch. It was Zoe's dad all right, you could tell, she'd inherited his ears.

As Mr Trubshawe strode down the front path, we all leaped up and scooted round the corner of the house. Then he kicked open his front gate, came out on to the pavement and started walking in our direction!

666
Beware of the DOG

We all stepped back. All except for Matt, who was at the back twiddling his lens. Nat stepped back right into him. He fell over, grabbing the nearest thing to steady his fall. This happened to be Nat. She fell back too and grabbed Joanne, who grabbed Ed, who grabbed me.

By the time we'd all picked ourselves up, Mr Trubshawe had gone.

"What a gross person!" exclaimed Nat. She turned to Matt. "Did you get some shots?"

Matt nodded. "I also got some bruises," he groaned, rubbing his shins, shoulder and neck.

"Let's go and get the film developed then," said Nat, "so the photos will be ready for the first edition. Then I'd better get on and finalize my story."

It was as if Ed, Joanne and I weren't there.

"Excuse me," I said. "Aren't you forgetting something? This is *my* story!"

Nat shook her head, firmly. "*We're* the journalists," she said, nodding in Matt's direction. "You just write the problem page."

"OK then, this is *my* problem!"

"Look," said Nat, "Zoe's got problems with her boyfriend. What would a tweenie like you know about that sort of thing? You haven't even *got* a boyfriend, have you?"

And off they swanned, arm in arm.

"That's not fair!" called Joanne.

I started to go after them, but Ed pulled me back. "Nat's right," he said, quietly.

I could've thumped him. "What!"

"You *do* write the problem page. It's your job to sort out Zoe's problem. You're responsible for helping her. It's not your job to write the news items."

I couldn't believe it! Ed was agreeing with Nat 'n' Matt! "I thought *you'd* be on my side," I said. "Ali would've been."

I stormed off up the road.

"Wait for me, Stacey!" called Joanne.

I turned round. "Haven't you got to find a one-legged Eskimo or something?" I shouted.

I turned back and put my head down. It wasn't fair. Nothing was fair. There was only one person who would understand, and she was in London.

When I got in, I rang Ali's number.

There was no reply.

I picked up the post from the doormat. There was a letter addressed to me. Or, to be more accurate, it was addressed to Ms S. Stove. So, unless someone had taken to writing to our gas cooker, I reckoned it was probably for me. Then I noticed the bright red, embossed *Wake Up World!* logo in the top lefthand corner of the envelope. I tore it open.

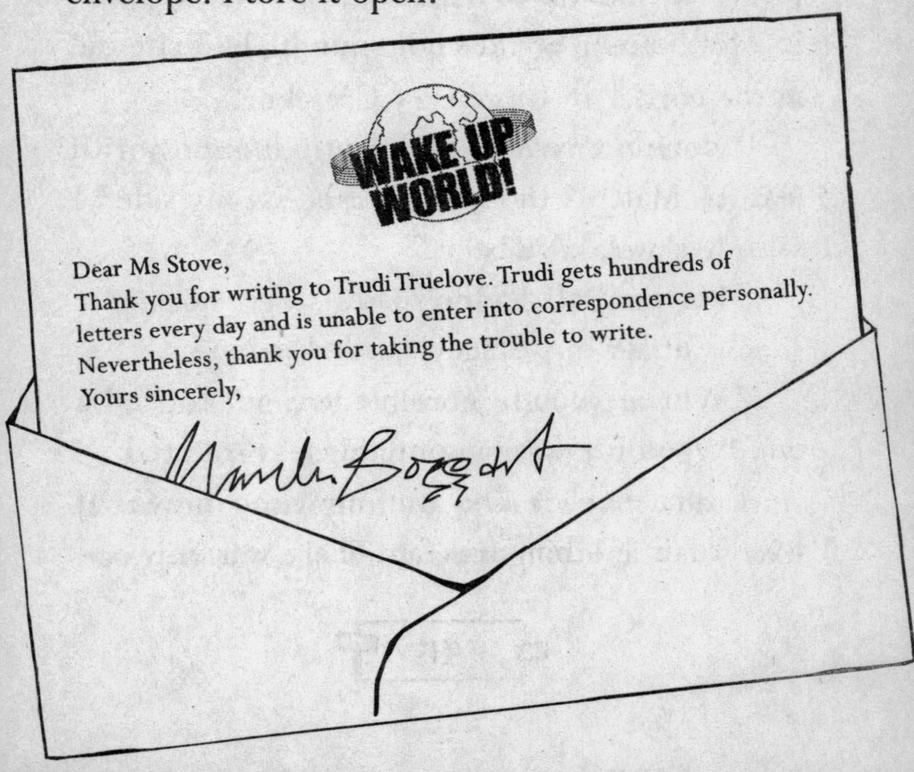

Marcia Boggart, I thought? Who on earth is Marcia Boggart?

"Production Secretary, *Wake Up World!*" said the letter.

There was only one suitable place for a letter from Marcia Boggart. I scrunched it into a ball, dropped it down the toilet and flushed it away. Honestly! What was the point of an agony aunt who didn't "enter into correspondence". Agony aunts were there to help people with their problems. It made me realize that Ed was right. My job *was* to help Zoe.

Next morning, I caught up with him as usual at the corner of Cranberry Crescent.

"Notice anything different about me?" I asked him.

He shook his head.

"I've lost my shadow," I said. "See, no sign of Joanne at all!"

"Why are you so horrible to her?" said Ed.

"Wouldn't you be, if you were me?" I retorted. "She's taken to following me about like she's a lost puppy. And she's a copycat.

Always agreeing with me."

"She just wants to be part of things," Ed said.

"She gives me the creeps!" I declared

Ed looked at me slowly and deliberately. "You mean, she's not Ali."

"Of course she's not Ali! Ali is my best friend!"

"*Was* your best friend," Ed said. "But now she's moved to London, and it's no good being angry with Joanne about it."

"I am not angry!" I shouted. "Anyway, what would you understand about it all? You're a boy. Boys don't have best friends."

I raced off up the road, leaving Ed standing. Deep down, of course, I knew he was right. I was angry about losing my best friend. And I was being mean to Joanne. That's Ed's trouble. He *is* right, most of the time. It's a very annoying habit. Especially in a boy.

At break-time, I caught up with Zoe in the playground.

"Hi!" I said.

"Hi," said Zoe, looking around to make sure

no one was watching her talking to me, a mere Year 7. I tried not to look bothered. After getting the cold shoulder from Nat 'n' Matt, I was getting rather used to knowing what it felt like to be a diseased person.

"Got your e-mail," I said.

"Right," said Zoe. She looked around again. "You've haven't told anyone else about it?" she asked, anxiously.

"No! Course not!" I replied indignantly. Then, remembering what Ed had said about me being responsible, I added, "Ah ... er ... except the editorial board."

"Nat 'n' Matt?" whispered Zoe in horror.

"Don't worry," I said, trying to sound convincing. "They take their responsibilities as editors very seriously. I can promise you, they won't blab."

Zoe seemed reassured. "If you say so, Stacey." She paused. "And so ... you will help me?"

"Of course I'll help you, Zoe!" I said.

A weight seemed to lift from Zoe's

shoulders. You could hear the relief in her breath. "Thank you," she whispered. "You do understand? Brad ... I do love him so."

"Of course I understand," I said. It seemed the right thing to say. "Don't worry," I added. "We'll get your dad to see sense."

Zoe beamed a big smile. "Thanks, Stacey!" she said. "You're a star." And she trotted off to join a couple of her mates, who were busy practising the steps to the latest S Club 7 single. She glanced back in my direction. She was still smiling.

I felt a lump rising in my throat. Zoe trusted me to solve her problem. I was responsible. I'd got to help her now, whatever it took. It's amazing what being called "a star" can do to you.

I thought hard about my next course of action. I had to do the right thing: Zoe's happiness – and Brad's life – depended on it.

It was time to enlist Ed's help. I stared long and hard at the ground. It wouldn't be hard to find him. There was a trail of crisps, leading out of the playground...

The X, Y and Z Files

As I'd suspected, I found Ed at the end of the crisp trail. He was sitting with his back up against one of the compost bins we'd used for our Recycling Project last year. He appeared to be studying the hole in the bottom of his Family Economy-size crisp packet. Surely, he hadn't come here in search of scraps of food? I was going to ask him, then thought better of it.

"Ed!"

"What?"

"I want to ask you a favour."

"You're not having any of my crisps!"

"I don't want any of your crisps," I sighed.

"Good."

"I want you to e-mail the United Nations in Geneva."

"What?"

I decided flattery was the best route. It usually is, when it comes to boys.

"You were right, Ed."

"Yeah." Ed nodded.

"What do you mean, yeah? You don't even know what it is I'm saying you were right about."

"I'm often right about things," said Ed, with a shrug. "At least, I'm often righter than *you* about things."

"What things?" I asked him, crossly.

"The thing you've just told me I'm right about, for a start," said Ed.

Honestly! You know scientists think there is this parallel universe that exists alongside ours? Well, Ed lives there.

"Listen," I said, firmly. "I've been thinking about what you said, about it being my responsibility to help Zoe. I think you're right and I think Zoe's got a right to see Brad."

"Good," said Ed. "But what's the United Nations got to do with it?"

"Haven't you ever heard of the United Nations Children's Charter?" I said. "There's a clause in it about people being free to choose their own friends."

"Is there?"

"Oh, for goodness' sake," I snapped. "You can be so picky sometimes. There's bound to be! It's a fundamental right, isn't it? Well, Zoe's dad's in breach of it. And that's illegal."

"So's putting someone in a sack and chucking them in the river," replied Ed.

"I know, I know. But Zoe's problem is really two problems. One, to make sure her dad doesn't kill Brad, and two, to make sure that her dad allows her to see him. Once her dad receives a visit from a couple of high-powered UN lawyers, he'll soon change his mind."

"And you really think the United Nations will be interested in Zoe's problem?" Ed asked.

"Of course they will!" I replied.

"Then why don't *you* email them, then?" said Ed, frowning. "You're the agony aunt."

"Because *you're* the foreign correspondent," I pointed out. "Besides, I shall be busy after school, sorting out the first bit of Zoe's problem."

"And how are you going to do that?" asked Ed.

"I'm going to talk to the police."

Ed raised an eyebrow. "Are you sure that's a good idea?"

"I've got to," I said, evenly. "I can't betray Zoe's trust. I've promised to stop her dad from murdering Brad. Anyway, I'm not worried about going to a police station. I know what they're like."

"Do you?" asked Ed.

"Course. I've seen inside a police station zillions of times."

"When?"

"On *The Bill*, of course!"

I wasted no time. Straight after school I made my way to the police station in the centre of town.

I pushed open the plate-glass door and had my first shock. Sun Hill? Not. In fact, it was more like a chip shop than a cop shop. The only things inside the tiny room were a couple of broken fold-up chairs and one of those lift-up counters.

A police officer came through from a door behind the counter, and that was when I got my second shock. He was old enough to be my grandad, no, my *great*-grandad. I mean I know the police are nicknamed the "Old Bill", but this guy was *Ancient* Bill.

He looked at me briefly, then placed a pink form he was holding on the counter in front of him. The heading said: LOST PROPERTY.

Without looking up, Officer Plod said, "Right miss, shall we get started?"

I'd never been called "miss" before, and I was determined I wasn't going to start being called "miss" now.

"*Ms*," I replied.

"Right, Miss Muzz," said the officer, scribbling the name down on his form. "Bike, budgie or Barbie doll?"

"Sorry?"

This time the officer looked up and sighed, deeply. "What is it you've lost? A bike, a budgie or a Barbie doll...?"

"What?"

I could not believe it! First, he had called me "miss" and now he was insinuating that I played with Barbie dolls! Couldn't he see that I was twelve years old? Twelve years and eleven days, to be precise? He was meant to be a police officer, for goodness' sake! He was meant to be observant!

Before I could explain, he was off again. "Bikes and budgies disappear on a regular basis throughout the year, but Barbie dolls are particular targets for theft in the months running up to Christmas. Hundreds of them go missing, then turn up down at the market or at car-boot sales."

As the police officer paused to take a breath, I finally managed to get a word in.

"I haven't lost anything," I protested. "I've come to report a murder."

"Oh." The police officer frowned. "Haven't got a form for that." He took a sheet of plain white paper and wrote MURDER in big capital letters along the top. "So, when did this murder take place?"

"It hasn't – yet," I replied.

"Ah," said Officer Plod.

Carefully, I explained how a man I called X was going to pop a boy, who I called Y, into a sack and chuck him into the river, because he was going out with his daughter – whom I called Z. Then I realized that Z was the first letter of Zoe and might give him a clue to her identity, so I told him the story again, calling Zoe X, Zoe's dad Y and Brad Z.

The police officer held up a hand. "One moment, Miss Muzz. Can you give me some names?"

I shook my head. "I'm afraid I can't.

BEWARE
POLICE
POLICE
MURDER
LOST

You see, I'm an agony aunt. I run a problem page for our school newspaper. It's called *The Grundy Times*."

Officer Plod frowned.

"Oh, you won't have heard of the paper yet," I explained, "the first edition isn't out till the end of next week."

"So why does being an agony aunt prevent you from giving me some names?" the officer asked me.

"These names have been given to me in confidence. It's a bit like being a priest," I explained, trying not to think about all the people who already knew about Zoe.

The police officer scratched his moustache. "Well," he muttered, "as no crime has been committed—"

"Yet," I reminded him.

"As no crime has been committed," he repeated, a little more tetchily, "this is really a matter for the Crime Prevention Officer."

"Then can I see the Crime Prevention Officer, please?" I asked.

The police officer shook his head. "I'm afraid not. He couldn't get in today." Officer Plod winced. "His patrol car's been stolen."

"So there's nothing you can do to help?"

Officer Plod shook his head. "Not without some names."

"So, I'll come back when the murder's taken place, shall I?" I asked, rapidly beginning to understand just why it was that people took the law into their own hands.

The police officer nodded, slowly.

"In that case," I told him, "it's a good job my friend is getting the United Nations in on the case, isn't it?"

And I turned on my heel and walked out of the station without so much as a backward glance.

I just hoped I'd be there to see the police officer's face when a team of crack lawyers from the United Nations turned up to question him.

The Dad Who Would Dare To Drown His Daughter's Darling!!!!!

My visit to the police station had been such a wash-out, I didn't bother to mention it to the others the next day. I didn't see much of Nat 'n' Matt anyway, thank goodness, because they were in Year 8. Joanne spent break time and dinner time telling me about her latest Swap Shop items – a copy of *Harry Potter and the Goblet of Fire* with the last twelve pages missing, and a tennis racket with no strings – and every time I saw Ed, he had his mouth full of food and couldn't speak.

It was about ten minutes to home time

when a small boy from Year 4 arrived with a message for Ms Angel. I didn't hear what the message was, I wasn't that interested, not until Ms Angel dismissed the small boy and turned her attention to Ed.

"Ed," she said. "Apparently there's someone from the United Nations to see you in the school office."

"What?" asked Ed.

Ms Angel repeated the message. Ed leaped to his feet. So did I.

"Stacey, your name isn't Ed," frowned Ms Angel.

"No, miss, but it's to do with me and my problem page," I explained.

Ms Angel looked to Ed for guidance.

"Yeah, it *is* to do with Stacey's problem page," said Ed.

"OK," said Ms Angel, "maybe you'd better go along, too."

I put my things away and grabbed my bag. Then I noticed that Joanne was doing the same.

"What are you doing, Joanne?" asked

Ms Angel. "Are you working on Stacey's problem page, too?" Joanne looked from Ed to Ms Angel.

"Not exactly," she said.

"But it *is* to do with Joanne, too," said Ed. "She helped me write the e-mail to the United Nations."

Quite what Ed was playing at, asking Joanne to help him with the e-mail, I didn't know. He was a journalist. Writing was his business. A simple e-mail shouldn't have been beyond him.

"She corrected my spellings," said Ed.

My question was answered. Joanne was a good speller. I knew that from sitting next to her in class.

"Quite a little team, aren't you?" said Ms Angel.

"Yes!" said Joanne, smiling.

"Best of luck!" called Ms Angel.

"It was a brilliant idea of yours to write to the United Nations," said Joanne, as we marched down the corridor.

I didn't answer her. I was much too busy

wondering about the United Nations lawyers. How many of them would there be? What nationality would they be? Would they speak English? Would they be wearing their wigs and gowns?

Ed pushed open the door to the school office. We all stopped and stared.

There was just the one person sitting there. She had a wig on, all right. It was grey and slightly crooked. But a lawyer she was not. She was wearing a pale green mac, thick brown stockings and lace-up shoes. And the frames of her glasses had been repaired with sticking plaster.

"Ah," she said to Ed, in a thin, reedy voice, "you must be Mr Reekie."

Ed nodded.

"I'm Miss Golightly. Your e-mail to the United Nations has been forwarded to me. I'm the secretary of your local United Nations Association. We support the work of the United Nations agencies locally. Particularly its work with children and refugees," she confided.

I was wondering if you and your young friends would care to take tea with me—"

"Thank you very much," said Ed, eagerly, never one to turn down the chance of free food.

"Shall we say Saturday? I'll be able to tell you more about our work, then. And we can talk about your friend's little problem too. Now, I must go, I've run out of cat litter and I've got to call into the pet shop on my way home."

She handed Ed a small card. "Here's my address. Shall we say three o'clock?" And with that, she trotted out into the playground and disappeared amongst the screaming masses who were streaming out of school like a herd of stampeding cattle.

Ed, Joanne and I made our way to the practical area, where Nat 'n' Matt had called another editorial meeting.

"Who does that old biddy think we are," I snorted, indignantly, "the Famous Five? There's a murder about to be committed and all she – and you for that matter – can think about," I added, giving Ed one of my withering looks, "is cake!"

"That's not true," said Ed. "I was thinking about sandwiches and chocolate biscuits too!"

"Oh, very funny," I said. "Great lot of help you are."

"She said she'd talk about our friend's little problem," said Joanne.

"Talk about it? You can't *talk* about murder. You have to *stop* it," I replied.

"Perhaps she's a detective," Joanne went on, "an old lady detective, like the one on the telly."

Sometimes I think I'm the only sane person in the world.

The door to the practical area was locked. We hung about for quarter of an hour, then Nat 'n' Matt strolled up with the key. They were making a point. And the point was: we're in charge, you dummies. Both of them wore superior smiles, which I didn't like. This wasn't a *new* expression for them – they *always* wore superior smiles which I didn't like – but these superior smiles were extra *knowing*.

When we went into the practical area, I saw exactly why.

There, pulsating away in glorious techni-colour on the computer monitor, was Nat 'n' Matt's *new* front page mock-up of *The Grundy Times*.

THE GRUNDY TIMES

THE DAD WHO WOULD DARE TO DROWN HIS DAUGHTER'S DARLING

We reveal heartbroken Zoe's tearful anguish!

see pages 2, 3, 4, 5 & 6

"Good, isn't it?" said Matt. He and Nat smiled at each other.

I thought of Zoe. "You're not using it," I said, quietly.

"Oh?" snapped Nat. "What's wrong with it?

Except for the fact that you weren't bright enough to think of it?"

"It's tacky and sick and Zoe would be devastated," I replied.

Nat shrugged. "So what's wrong with it?"

"You're not using it," I repeated.

"Excuse me," said Nat, thrusting her shoulders back, "but *we're* the editors."

"And I'm the agony aunt," I said. "Zoe wrote to me – in confidence."

"Then you rather let the cat out of the bag, didn't you?" Matt smirked.

"I gave her my word you wouldn't blab the story about!" I was shouting now.

"You're not responsible for the front page. We are," Nat replied, firmly.

"Responsible? You're not responsible!"

"Don't you care about the effect that page could have on Zoe?" Joanne asked Nat.

"I'm a newspaper editor, not a social worker," retorted Nat.

"Haven't you got any morals at all?" Joanne shouted.

"Of course she hasn't. You heard her. She's a newspaper editor," muttered Ed, through a mouthful of crisps.

"We're going with it," said Nat.

"If you do, I'll…" I began and stopped myself. But it was too late.

"What?" beamed Nat, triumphantly. "Resign? Oh good. I've already got a letter of resignation typed out here. All you've got to do is sign it."

Nat thrust a neatly laid-out letter into my hand. It was short, if not particularly sweet:

> Dear Natalie and Matthew,
>
> I hereby tender my resignation from the post of agony aunt on **The Grundy Times**. I do not wish to be involved with **The Grundy Times** in any way ever again, either.
>
> Yours sincerely
>
> **(SIGN HERE!)**
>
> Stacy Stone

And she'd spelled my name wrong!

"Here's a pen," Nat said, with a twisted little smile.

I stood there, my cheeks burning. Nat had planned this, and she'd got me just where she wanted me. To keep my job on the paper I would have to drop Zoe in the deepest doo-dah imaginable – and break my promise to her.

I was about to give in when the phone rang. Ed swallowed a mouthful of crisps and answered it.

"Wit's wor woo." He handed me the phone.

"Hello," I said. "Stacey here."

It was Zoe. I was aware of the others all looking at me. Joanne and Nat 'n' Matt sat perfectly still, as if they'd just started a game of Statues. Ed carried on munching his crisps.

Zoe managed to get her story out to me between sobs.

"He can't have done!" I said to her.

"What is it?" hissed Matt.

"No, surely not ... he wouldn't have!" I muttered.

"Stacey, what is it?" whispered Joanne.

"Will you promise me you'll stay there?" I said, as calmly as I could. "I'll sort something. Don't you worry." I put down the phone.

"Well?" asked Matt.

I waited for Nat to crack. It took about a nano-second.

"Stacey Stone, you pathetic poser!" she yelled. "Tell us!"

"That was Zoe," I said, calmly.

"We *know* it was Zoe," yelled everyone, including Ed, who also showered me with a mouthful of soggy, half-chewed crisps.

"She and Brad were up in her room and her dad came home from work early and found them together."

"And?" said Nat. She was really hooked now.

"And he told Zoe he's going to do for the little rat once and for all. He's locked him in the shed while he pops round to his mate's to borrow a sack and some house bricks."

Nobody said anything. The only sound was the slow, methodical crunch of Ed's teeth on his crisps.

I had to take control. Zoe had come to me for help and I was responsible for the situation. "The way I see it is this," I said. "Zoe has trusted me with her problem. The police and the United Nations won't do anything to help. So it's up to me. Both as an agony aunt and as a human being."

I caught Joanne's admiring look. Nat 'n' Matt looked puzzled, which was hardly surprising. I'd used words completely outside their vocabulary. Words like "human" and "being".

"So what are you going to do?" asked Ed, taking a break from his crisps.

"I'm going to the Trubshawes' right now. I'm going to release Brad from the shed and then I'm going to confront Mr Trubshawe," I explained. "If there's anyone who'd like to tag along, your support would be most welcome. If not, I'm quite happy to go in alone."

Joanne got up. "Of course you're not going in alone," she said.

Nat 'n' Matt got up. "We're right behind you," said Nat.

"No cameras," I said, firmly. "We don't want to antagonize him."

Matt nodded. All thoughts of me resigning had been forgotten. For the moment.

The one person whose support I would have liked most remained with his bottom in a comfy chair. "Are you coming?" I asked.

"Finish me crisps, first," said Ed.

The Man With HAT On His Fingers!

We stopped off at Matt's house while he went in for what he called "some cool gear". Having seen *Death Wish 3* six times, Matt claimed he was an expert on vigilante action and I half-expected him to appear with an armful of pump-action sub-machine guns. Instead, he came out of the house waving a couple of black berets and two pairs of sunglasses.

"We've got to look the part. Everyone knows vigilantes always wear berets and shades," he said.

"I'm not wearing a beret and shades," I said.

"I'm going in strictly as an agony aunt, and not as a vigilante."

"I'm not wearing them, either," said Joanne, predictably.

"Nor am I," muttered Ed, who had just caught us up.

"I wasn't going to offer them to you lot, anyway," snapped Matt. He placed one of the berets on Nat's head.

"It's lovely," she cooed, "matches my eye liner. Where did you get them?"

"They're my little brothers' St John's Ambulance Brigade berets," Matt explained. "They joined the St John's so they could get into football matches for free."

The two vigilantes, now cleverly disguised as first aiders, looked lovingly into each other's eyes. Though given that they were both wearing shades, they probably couldn't see very much.

As we set off towards the Trubshawes', Ed grabbed my arm and held me back.

"You sure you want to go through with this?" he hissed.

We had reached the far end of Zoe's road. Nat 'n' Matt marched on, completely unaware that we had stopped.

"I'm not sure I *want* to," I replied, "but I've certainly *got* to. I'm responsible, remember? That's what *you* told me. I'm an agony aunt. Zoe's problem is my problem."

"You'll know all about agony, by the time Old Man Trubshawe's done with you," muttered Ed. "You know he's got the letters H. A. T. tattooed on his knuckles?"

"Hat? That's funny. Don't you mean H. A. T. E?" said Joanne, pushing her way between us. Like I mentioned before, she's dead hot on spelling.

Ed nodded. "It used to say HATE, you're right, but Old Man Trubshawe lost his little finger."

"How careless of him," I murmured.

"What happened to it?" asked Joanne. I instantly wished she hadn't.

"Lassie, the Trubshawes' pet Rottweiler, bit it off," explained Ed.

"Thanks for that, Joanne," I muttered. "Now I feel heaps better."

Up ahead of us, Nat 'n' Matt had stopped. "Come on, you lot," yelled Matt. "We need to get to Zoe's before her dad comes back!"

"Thank you, Matt, for broadcasting our business to the whole of the street," I sighed.

We reached the Trubshawes' and I explained to the others what I had in mind. "I'll knock and see if Mr Trubshawe's back. If he's not, I'll get Zoe to take me round to the shed and then I'll free Brad. Only act if you see Mr Trubshawe coming back."

Ed, Nat 'n' Matt and Joanne took cover behind the hedge, while I went up to the front door.

I rang the doorbell. The first few notes of the *Brookie* theme tune filled the air.

Zoe opened the door, looking tearful.

"Hi Zoe," I said, "it's all right. I'm here to sort things out for you."

Zoe sniffed.

"Has your dad come back?"

"No," Zoe mumbled.

"Then let's go and rescue Brad!" I tried to sound chirpy, but I was so nervous. I was shivering and shaking about like a washing machine on a fast spin cycle.

I followed Zoe indoors.

"Dad's taken the shed key with him," Zoe sniffed.

"Then we'll have to force the door," I said.

"Right."

We went through to the kitchen and Zoe opened the cutlery drawer. Nestling next to a ladle and a pair of salad tongs were two crowbars and a club hammer.

"Dad's work tools," explained Zoe.

I could only think of one trade where your only tools were a crowbar and a club hammer: it rhymed with *gurgler*.

"Come on out to the garden," said Zoe, pushing open the back door.

She said "garden", but "war zone" or "waste tip" would have been more appropriate. There was a rusting fridge with no door, a smashed television set, old bikes, empty lager cans and other assorted rubbish. And chained to a concrete washing post was the Hound of the Baskervilles.

"That's Lassie," said Zoe.

"Grrrrrrrrrrr!" said Lassie, which I think roughly translated as, "Shall I bite 'er 'ead off now, Zoe?"

"She's a great big softie, really."

"I'll take your word for it," I replied, edging nervously round the washing post.

A doggie bowl the size of a wash basin stood nearby. I quickly peered into it – I just couldn't help myself – but I didn't see any fingers.

Zoe handed me the crowbar and I eased it into the gap between the shed door and the wall and pushed. There was the satisfying sound of ripping wood. I was just about to open the door and heroically rescue Brad from certain death, when I heard a furious yell behind us:

“Oi! What do you two little toerags think you’re doing in my shed?”

I spun round and found myself face-to-chest with Mr Trubshawe. And there was no doubt about it – there was hate all over his face and HAT all over his knuckles.

9

The Day A Hippopotamus Dropped From The Sky!

"Run!" screamed Zoe.

I didn't need telling twice. I ducked out of the way of Mr Trubshawe's outstretched hand and legged it back down the path after Zoe, towards the passage at the side of the house.

The shouting and the screaming had turned Lassie from a furtive beast into a frenzied one. She leaped into the air, snarling, baring her teeth and yanking at her lead. The concrete washing post vibrated alarmingly under the strain.

Zoe had already reached the back gate to the side passage and I was only a metre or so behind her. But then she made her fatal mistake. She glanced back to see how close her dad was to us. Unfortunately, the cavalry, in the form of Matt, Nat, Ed and Joanne, were charging through the gate in the other direction and she crashed headlong into Matt. Down they went, blocking my path. And down I went on top of them. Then something landed on top of me, knocking all the air from my lungs. Something heavy. In my terrified panic, my brain told me it could be either:

a: A hippopotamus – on its way from Africa to the local safari park – falling from the hold of a passing cargo aircraft.

OR

b: A Mr Trubshawe.

I suspected it was the latter.

Suddenly my left ear rang with the sound of a piercing cry of pain and the weight rolled off me. At first I thought it *was* a hippopotamus – one badly in need of a facelift – then I saw that it was indeed Mr Trubshawe.

The reason for the piercing cry of pain was that Joanne had her knee in the small of his back and was pulling at his lank hair with both hands.

"You leave Stacey alone," she yelled. "You cold-blooded murderer!"

As I struggled to my feet, my attention was suddenly drawn to another set of screams behind me.

"You get your filthy mitts off my bloke!" Nat was yelling at Zoe, who to be fair, was struggling to get off Matt.

Then another boy's voice shouted, "What you doing with my girlfriend, Pascoe?" And a pair of fists began pummelling Matt. The fists – and the voice – belonged to Simon Froggitt, from Year 8.

Suddenly, Nat sidestepped out of Zoe's path and gave me a shove. "This is all your fault, you twit-faced tweenie!" she screeched at me.

"Yeah! It is!" agreed Zoe, and she gave me a shove, too.

"Ed!" I yelled. "Help me!"

But Ed wasn't listening. He was looking up

the side passage towards the street. Half-a-dozen police officers in riot gear were bursting out of the back of a couple of police minibuses, waving their truncheons about their heads and heading up the Trubshawes' path towards us.

"It's all right, miss, we'll take over now!" the one in charge yelled to Joanne, who was still sitting on Mr Trubshawe with her knee in his back, pulling his hair.

At the sight of the riot police, Nat and Zoe stopped shoving me and quickly retired to the sidelines with Ed, Matt and Simon-Froggitt-from-Year-8.

Somewhat reluctantly, I thought, Joanne let go of Mr Trubshawe's hair and came over to join us. "I hope he gets life!" she hissed to the officer, her beady little eyes blazing.

"What do you think you're doing?" shouted Mr Trubshawe, as a couple of beefy officers grabbed his arms. "It's these kids you should be sorting out!"

As the police officers pulled Mr Trubshawe to his feet, another car drew up. A man in ordinary clothes climbed out and made his way towards us. He had silver hair and a severe, serious face. He looked dead important. As he approached us, all the other police officers turned to look at him. So did we. You couldn't *not* look at him; he had a sort of presence.

He walked up to Mr Trubshawe. There was complete silence.

"Donny Trubshawe!" He smiled triumphantly. "I've been waiting a long time for this moment. It looks like your number's up, sunshine!"

Mr Trubshawe's beetrooty face paled to a light pink. "Chief Inspector Moss," he stammered.

Chief Inspector Moss took a step closer to Mr Trubshawe and smiled. "Information we have received leads us to believe that—"

"Hold up," said Mr Trubshawe, defiantly. "You haven't got nothing on me. I was in *The Squashed Hedgehog* last night, drinking with my mates. You can't pin the Buckingham Hall burglary on me. I've got an alibi."

Chief Inspector Moss shook his head. "Buckingham Hall burglary? Who mentioned the Buckingham Hall burglary? The information we have received leads us to believe that you have detained a young person against their will with a view to wilful murder. You're looking at fifteen years, Donny."

Interesting though this all was, my mind was racing with other matters: someone had gone to the police about Zoe and Brad. I looked around at the suspects. Ed? Surely not. Joanne? Hardly. Nat 'n' Matt? It had to be! I glanced over at them. They were trying to look all innocent.

I couldn't believe it. I'd promised Zoe that I wouldn't tell a soul and now it seemed that the entire local police force knew. I waited for Zoe to explode, but when I dared to look her way, she was just standing there, looking up into her dad's eyes.

"Oh Dad, what have you done now?" she asked him, anxiously.

"I haven't murdered no one!" protested a worried Mr Trubshawe, his pink face now turning distinctly pasty. "I've been set up!"

Chief Inspector Moss continued to stare Mr Trubshawe out. "Does the name 'Brad' not mean anything to you, Mr Trubshawe?"

At the mere mention of the name, Mr Trubshawe flinched, and his face turned from pasty white to Persil white.

"Ah," said Chief Inspector Moss, with meaning.

"Zoe!" shouted Mr Trubshawe, suddenly angry. "This is all *your* doing, isn't it? Just because I wouldn't let that rat into my house, you've gone and set me up on a murder rap! I suppose you learned this sort of behaviour from your mother, didn't you?"

I looked at Zoe. She had the kind of blank, puzzled look of someone who didn't know what on earth was going on. And she wasn't the only one.

"The point is, Donny," said Chief Inspector Moss, still standing right in front of Mr Trubshawe, "where is Brad now?"

"I locked him in the shed," he muttered.

Chief Inspector Moss shouted, "Go, men! Go, go, go!"

And the men went. Two minibus-loads of them charged down the Trubshawes' back garden towards the shed.

"Not you two!" Chief Inspector Moss shouted at two officers who were wearing wet-suits, flippers and snorkels. "Your job is to drag the river if we need to! You'd better put Donny here in the back of the van. And make sure you put the handcuffs on him!"

As a still-protesting Mr Trubshawe was dragged off by the two frogmen, Chief Inspector Moss turned to me and asked, "Do you know why they're called frogmen? It's because they've got the bodies of men and the brains of frogs."

I smiled, politely.

Unfortunately, there was no time for me to tell him a joke back as, just then, the police officers got into the shed.

"No sign of the lad in here, sir!" one of them called across.

Chief Inspector Moss looked grim. "Then we shall have to drag the river," he said.

Suddenly Zoe spoke. "Lad? What lad?" she

asked. She had a weird kind of expression on her face, like she suspected this wasn't really happening to her, and that it was all just a particularly bad dream.

"Brad," I reminded her, gently and calmly. "They're looking for Brad, your boyfriend. It seems as if your dad got to him before we did."

"No, you idiot!" shouted Zoe, impatiently. "Brad isn't my boyfriend. Simon Froggitt's my boyfriend!"

"Oh," said Chief Inspector Moss. "Well then, just who is Brad?"

With an eerie sense of timing, one of the officers in the shed called out, "The only living thing we can find in here is a white rat in a cage!"

"Brad!" yelled Zoe.

"Brad?" echoed Chief Inspector Moss.

All of a sudden there were knots in my stomach and jelly in my legs as the awful truth began to dawn on me.

Chief Inspector Moss took a deep breath. "So, let me get this straight. This Brad your father was threatening to drown in the river was not a person, but this pet rodent?"

"Yes!" said Zoe, clutching hold of a cage containing one white pet fancy rat. "He wouldn't let me keep him in my room!"

"So who rang us with the information that Mr Trubshawe was about to murder your boyfriend?" asked Chief Inspector Moss.

Zoe stared at me down her nose as if I was some primitive form of pond life. Nat 'n' Matt, Joanne and Ed were all staring at me, too. Nat ran her finger all the way along her neck in a friendly "I'm-gonna-kill-yer" way.

"It wasn't me!" I protested.

A furious-looking Chief Inspector Moss yelled across to the frogmen who were guarding Mr Trubshawe. "OK, men! You can let him go."

Mr Trubshawe tumbled out of the back of the van and lurched down the side path towards us. "I'm going to sue you lot," he yelled at the police officers. "Wrongful arrest. Blackening my good name."

"But you haven't got a good name, Dad," said Zoe.

"Well, now! All's well that ends well!" I said, hopefully.

Zoe's eyes were blazing. "This is *not* the end!" she said. "You promised you wouldn't let *them* tell!" She scowled at Nat 'n' Matt. "Now the whole school's going to know!"

She took Brad from his cage and stroked him between the ears. Mr Trubshawe shivered and took a step back. I just stood there. I couldn't think of anything to say, I felt so bad.

Chief Inspector Moss was consulting his notebook. "Wasting police time is a serious offence," he was saying. "Luckily, we've got the name of the person who rang in with the information that Mr Trubshawe here was about to commit murder. Fellow by the name of Pascoe. Matthew Pascoe."

"Matt!" gasped Nat, in alarm.

A police constable sidled up to Chief Inspector Moss. "Do you want us to bring him down the station and fling the book at him, sir?"

"Oh no," said Chief Inspector Moss. "Mr Trubshawe here can take care of him."

"Yeah, you wait till I get my hands on the toerag," seethed Mr Trubshawe.

"But … it wasn't me!" stammered Matt, who had gone as white as a sheet and was hiding behind Nat.

"No, he's right, it couldn't have been him!" Nat pointed out with some passion. "He's not been out of our sight all afternoon, has he, Stacey?"

What could I do but back Nat up? "No," I agreed. "He hasn't."

"Then whoever rang the police must have used his name," reasoned Chief Inspector Moss. He paused and scanned all our faces. "Any idea who that might have been?" he asked.

I glanced around at the rest of our group.

Ed was nowhere to be seen.

10

Furious Head Bans School Newspaper!

After some severe words, Chief Inspector Moss told us that he wasn't going to arrest us. Instead, he would be informing the school about our irresponsible behaviour.

After that, Nat 'n' Matt slunk off home – not without a few fiery looks in my direction. Joanne wanted to walk home with me, of course, but I made an excuse. I just wanted to be alone.

I watched telly all evening.

I didn't leave the house all weekend. On Saturday I stayed in bed. The only sounds I heard all day were the piercing shrieks that came from Lena's bedroom as she plucked her eyebrows.

That and the telephone ringing. Twelve times in all. Eleven of those times it was Lena's best friend Jasmine. Jasmine lives just over the road from us. They seemed to have a lot of dead important things to discuss like bra sizes, hair-removing cream and Geography homework.

On the other occasion the phone went, Lena yelled through my door, "It's for you, Miss Mopey! Someone called Joanne."

"Tell her I'm not here, zit-face!" I shouted back.

I heard her yell down the phone, "She says she's not here, zit-face!"

On Sunday we went to my gran's. I watched telly there all day, too.

By Monday morning, I was feeling so terrible I seriously thought about skipping school. I certainly felt sick to the bottom of my stomach. But then I'd only have to make up another excuse for Tuesday and then yet another for Wednesday and then there would be

Thursday … I worked out that if I was going to avoid school till I could officially leave at sixteen, I'd have to invent one thousand three hundred and sixty-five excuses. That was too many excuses, even for a brilliantly imaginative person like me.

As it was, I ended up getting to school really early. I decided it was better that way. Less chance of bumping into any of the others.

I'd only got one foot inside the school doors when Mrs Dickens, the school secretary, rapped on her little sliding glass window.

"Mr Pook wishes to see you, Stacey!" she trilled. "Wait outside his office please."

There are four green sofa chairs outside Spooky Pooky's room for troublemakers and parents to sit on while they wait. I plonked myself down. Pretty soon, Joanne joined me.

"I tried to phone you on Saturday," she said. "You missed tea with Miss Golightly."

"Bet that was a thrilling experience," I replied.

"Don't feel so bad," she said. "Anybody

could've made the same mistake." She smiled what I presume she thought was a sympathetic smile, but it only made me feel worse.

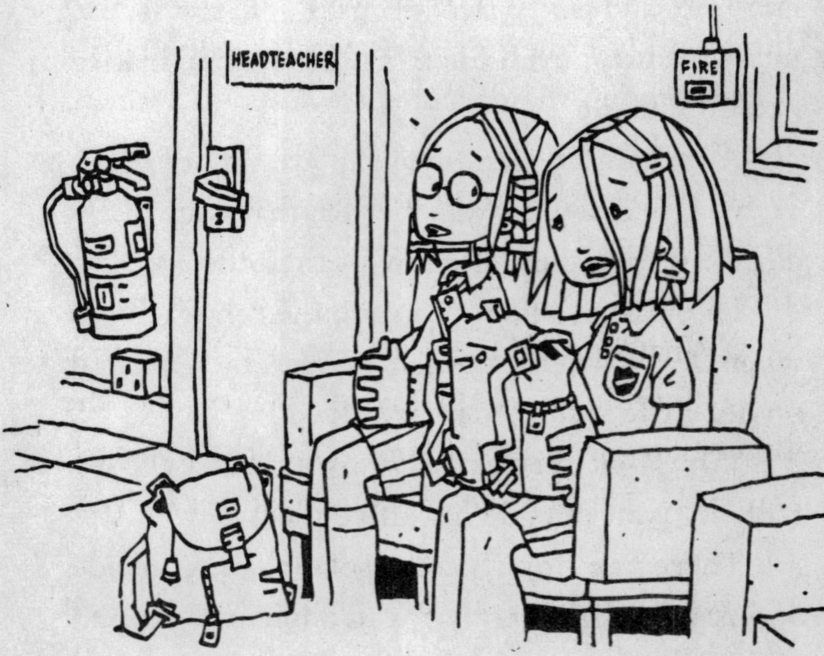

"Anybody could not have made the same mistake," spat a voice behind us. Nat – and Matt – had arrived. "It's a peculiar sort of thicko who can't distinguish between a pet fancy rat and a Simon Froggitt."

"If you two are so-o-o-o-o-o clever, why

didn't you twig that Brad was Zoe's pet rat, eh?" said Joanne, firmly.

Nat was lost for words. So was I. It was a smart answer – for a Swap Shop compiler. Matt didn't reply either. He was busily watching Ed wandering up the corridor towards us, munching on a bit of toast.

"Ed Reekie? Did you make that call to the police using my name?" he demanded, threateningly.

"What?" said Ed.

Before Matt could say another word, the door flew open and Spooky Pooky appeared. "Come!" he sneered at us out of the corner of his mouth.

Ms Angel was already there. She did not look happy.

We shuffled into a bedraggled line in front of Spooky Pooky's desk and hung our heads.

"I warned Ms Angel that a school newspaper written by children would only lead to trouble, didn't I, Ms Angel?"

Ms Angel nodded.

"A parent of a child in this school has been slandered. Two vanloads of highly-trained police officers and two frogmen have been called out on a false alarm. The good name of The Doris Grundy Middle School has been dragged through the mud. And all because of *The Grundy Times*! As I have just informed Ms Angel, the paper, which I should never have allowed you to take over in the first place, will be shut down with immediate effect."

There was a short gasp from Nat.

Spooky Pooky stood up and glowered down at us. "I must admit I'm surprised at you, Natalie and Matthew," he said, "for being so easily influenced by your younger and more irresponsible colleagues." Here he cast a withering look in my direction. "Quite what the Director of Education will say when she hears about this debacle, I can't bear to imagine."

There was a knock at the door and Mrs Dickens marched in. "Sorry to interrupt you, Mr Pook," she said, "but there's a soldier waiting in the school office, who wants to know how long this meeting will last."

Spooky Pooky clutched the sides of his desk and sat down heavily. Ms Angel poured him a glass of water.

"I have heard of schools where things are so out of hand that the government has brought in a private firm to run things," he said. "But this must be the only school in the country where things are so bad that the government has decided to send in the army!"

"Oh, he hasn't come to run the school," replied Mrs Dickens, lightly, "he's come for Ed."

"What?" said Ed.

"The police must've found out *you* made that call," said Matt, with a satisfied smirk

"Oh, and there's a little old lady with him," said Mrs Dickens.

"Oh, that'll be Miss Golightly, I expect," said Ed. "Yeah, she said she'd try and drop by the school."

"Who," enquired Spooky Pooky, in an exasperated voice, "is Miss Golightly?"

"She's a United Nations person," said Ed.

"Joanne and I went to her place for tea on Saturday."

"Why has she brought a soldier to school with her?" asked Ms Angel.

Spooky Pooky sighed and turned to Mrs Dickens. "Don't you think it would be a good idea to show Miss Golightly and the Army officer along to my office now, to see if they can shed any light upon this matter?" he muttered. Which I thought, for a head teacher, was a pretty intelligent suggestion.

Five minutes later, Miss Golightly and the soldier joined us in Spooky Pooky's office. The soldier's name was Captain Smith-Jones. He was quite young, *very* fit and he had these lovely pale-blue eyes, which matched his beret.

He explained to everyone that he'd been peace-keeping in Kosovo and now he was back home, doing a tour of United Nations Associations and talking about his work and stuff.

"I was so impressed with what Ed was telling me at tea on Saturday about the responsibilities of being a Foreign Correspondent," Miss Golightly explained. "So I thought I'd bring Captain Smith-Jones along to your school, so that he and rest of you young newspaper people could talk to him. Did you finish all those cakes when you got home, Ed?"

"Yes, thank you," said Ed, "they were really tasty."

Miss Golightly smiled. "The point is," she continued, "Captain Smith-Jones is setting up a pen-pal club, through the United Nations, so that girls – and boys – in Kosovo can write to girls and boys here. And we wondered if Doris Grundy Middle School would like to get involved?"

The captain passed Miss Golightly a folder. From it she took out a black-and-white photograph and a letter in an envelope. The photograph was of a girl, about thirteen, with deep-set eyes and a sparkling face. Matt and Ed fell over themselves trying to get a closer look. Nat shot Matt a filthy look, but it didn't seem to have any effect.

"This is Katya. She lives in Pristina, in Kosovo. Like many of her classmates she lost her home in the recent war. Others have lost their friends or family, too," explained Miss Golightly.

Suddenly, problems with pet rats, boyfriends – even best friends who had moved away – didn't seem such a big deal after all. I tried to imagine how it must feel to come home from school and find your home demolished; your family dead.

"Katya and the rest of her class would love to have British pen-pals," Miss Golightly added. She turned to Spooky Pooky. "You must be very proud of these young people and their interest in world affairs," she said. "They're a credit to your school!"

"Are they?" said Spooky Pooky, doubtfully.

Ms Angel clapped her hands. "Well," she said. "I think we have a super newspaper headline in this Kosovo pen-pal story, don't you, Mr Pook?"

"You seem to forget, Ms Angel," replied Spooky Pooky, tetchily, "that there is no newspaper—"

"Oh, there certainly is!" Miss Golightly interrupted him. "Ed told me all about it. It's called *The Grundy Times*. I'm surprised you don't know about it, Mr Pook, being the head teacher here. I, for one, can't wait to see the first edition!" she added, excitedly.

"And neither can I," added Captain Smith-Jones.

If Spooky Pooky had been a kettle, there would have been steam coming out of his ears. He was in no position to argue. Not when we had the United Nations and the Army on our side.

"In the circumstances," he muttered through clenched teeth, "*The Grundy Times* can stay open—"

Nat 'n' Matt, Ed, Joanne and I let out a small cheer. Spooky Pooky doesn't like cheers. Not even small ones.

"Providing," he continued, "there are no more disgraceful incidents involving parents, pet rats and police frogmen!"

We all tried to look humble. But somehow, I don't think we managed it.

Agony Aunt Threatened With United Nations Sanctions!

At morning break there was an emergency meeting with the Editors From Hell. This suited me fine. It meant there was a good chance I could avoid bumping into Zoe. I was sure that she was still waiting to go ballistic at me for breaking my promise about keeping quiet. And who could blame her?

"Ed Reekie, you rang the police using my name, didn't you?" Matt growled, as soon as Ed strolled in.

Ed took an apple from his pocket and bit into it. "You make that accusation again,

Matt Pascoe and I'll resign from the paper, taking the Kosovo story with me. No lead story, no *Grundy Times*."

"I don't care!" fumed Matt.

"Yes, you do, Matt," snapped Nat. "You want to edit this paper with me, don't you?"

"Zoe's dad might've killed me, 'cos of him!" protested Matt, sulkily.

"Don't you, Matt?" repeated Nat, more loudly this time.

"Yeah," muttered Matt.

"Good," said Nat. "I don't know why you're making such a fuss."

Nat turned to me. "The real reason I called this emergency editorial meeting," she said grandly, "is that I think Stacey should resign. In view of the fact that she almost got us closed down."

I would've said something, but I didn't feel on very strong ground. There was a silence that seemed to last for ages. Then Joanne spoke. "If Stacey goes, I go," she said, firmly.

"So much the better," snapped Nat.

"Look," said Ed, quietly, "if Stacey hadn't had the idea of a problem page, there wouldn't have been an e-mail from Zoe Trubshawe, and if there hadn't been an e-mail from Zoe Trubshawe there wouldn't have been a visit from Miss Golightly, and if there hadn't been a visit from Miss Golightly—"

"OK, OK, you've made your point," said Nat, grumpily. I think Ed's speech was making her brain hurt. She huffed. She sighed. "You can stay on the team, Stacey. For now."

"Thanks," I said.

"Don't thank me, thank your little pals, here," she snorted.

"Thanks, Ed." I paused. "Thanks Joanne," I said.

I left Ed writing his Kosovo article and Joanne sorting out her Swap Shop items. I'd decided I just wanted to be quiet for a bit. I was heading across the playground, towards the loos, when I heard a voice yell:

"Stacey!"

I turned round and there was Zoe, arm in

arm with Simon Froggitt. There was no way out, so I decided to get in with my apology first.

"Zoe," I said. "I'm so, so sorry—"

She frowned. "What about?"

"That I broke my promise," I said, "about keeping your problem quiet."

"Oh. Right," said Zoe, breezily. "It doesn't matter now. It's worked out really cool. My dad was so pleased that the police ended up looking like prize bananas, he's going to let me keep Brad in my room, after all. Providing I promise to put a double lock on his cage."

"A double lock on his cage?"

"Yeah. Dad's terrified Brad will get out. He's scared senseless of rats. That's why he didn't like me keeping him indoors." She looked at me, guiltily. "I suppose that's why I got Brad in the first place. Just to tease him."

I gawped. "Your dad? Terrified of *rats*? But he's got HAT tattooed on his fingers!"

"So? That doesn't mean he's not a very sensitive person."

"Er, no. I suppose not," I agreed.

"So, thanks, Stacey. You promised we'd get my dad to see sense. And we did."

"I'm not sure I did anything much," I shrugged. "I got it all wrong."

"No, you didn't!" said Zoe. "Oh, you may have got the bit about Brad being a rat rather than a boy wrong, but you got the important bit right."

"Did I?"

"Yes! You believed me when I said I loved Brad. Most people would have said, 'Don't be stupid, how can anyone love a pet rat?' "

I had to agree, she had a point.

"Not only that, you made me believe things could get sorted," Zoe went on.

"I did?" I asked. I was beginning to enjoy the way this little chat was going.

"Yes! I thought, if someone like Stacey Stone, who's never even met Brad and who is only a Year 7 tweenie, is willing to take on my dad, then so am I! That's the only reason I had the nerve to ask Dad if he'd think again about Brad staying in my room."

"Right," I said.

"You won't tell anyone about my dad being scared of rats, will you?" Zoe added, suddenly.

"No, I promise," I replied. "This is one secret Nat 'n' Matt won't get to hear about."

"Good," said Zoe, "'Cos he'd kill you if you did."

She gave Simon Froggitt a big hug and they

headed off through the door and into school. I stood there, thinking about things. I thought I'd really messed up Zoe's problem, but she seemed to think I'd done all right. It was funny, the way things could work out.

Ed wandered over, finishing off an apple. "What are you doing?" he asked.

"Thinking," I said.

"That's a bit of a novelty, isn't it?"

I pretended not to have heard. "Ed...?"

"What?"

"People are quite complicated, aren't they? I mean, you think they're going to react in one way and they turn out to do something completely different."

"How do you mean?"

"Like, I bet when you made that cheeky remark then, you thought I was going to shove that apple core down the back of your shirt, didn't you?"

"The thought did cross my mind, yes."

"Well, I'm not."

"Good."

"I'm going to shove it down the *front* of your shirt."

I grabbed the apple core with my right hand and Ed's shirt with my left.

"Get off!" yelled Ed. "I'll get the United Nations on to you, I will!"

12

STOP PRESS!

The following week there was only one e-mail for me:

Dear Best Agony Aunt Ever,

My boyfriend's threatened to
chuck me 'cos my pet rat Brad bit
his ear. He says I've got to choose
between him and Brad.
What shall I do?

It wasn't signed. It didn't really need to be. Even if I hadn't recognized the address, trubshawe@freemail.com, I would've known it was from Zoe. I replied:

> Hi Zoe,
> Stick with Brad. If your boyfriend can't put up with a small inconvenience like having his ear bitten off, he obviously doesn't really love you.
>
> Kind regards
> Best Agony Aunt Ever.

The next day, Joanne got this advert for her Swap Shop column:

> Attractive Year 8 girl with sense of humour wants to swap old boyfriend for a new one. Must be gorgeous and like Steps and pet rats. ZT.

I was dead chuffed. It's pretty cool running a problem page. Especially when someone calls you "the best agony aunt ever".

Even more especially when someone takes your advice.

Yes, there was no doubt about it, I felt ready to take on any problems the readers of *The Grundy Times* might care to throw at me. And I couldn't help wondering just what that next problem would be...

Visit Roy Apps's web site!

Look out for the
BBC Scotland production of
Stacey Stone on BBC1!

CHECK OUT
THE
ZONE
SCHOLASTIC
www.scholastic.co.uk/zone
for the coolest books everyone's reading.